LEE COUNTY LIBRARY
107 Hawkins Ave.
Sanford, NC 27330

His Dogness
Finds a
Blue Heart

by Kim Underwood

Illustrations by Garnet Goldman

Copyright © 2004 by Ralph Kim Underwood
All rights reserved under
International and Pan-American Copyright Conventions.

The paper in this book meets the guidelines
for permanence and durability of the Committee on
Production Guidelines for Book Longevity
of the Council on Library Resources.

Printed in Mexico

Design by Debra Long Hampton

Library of Congress Cataloging-in-Publication Data

Underwood, Ralph Kim, 1953-
His dogness finds a blue heart / by Ralph Kim Underwood ;
illustrations by Garnet Goldman.
        p.   cm.
    ISBN 0-89587-304-4 (alk. paper)
1. Dog owners–Fiction. 2. Heart–Fiction. 3. Dogs–Fiction. I.
    Title. PS3621.N387H57 2004
            813'.6--dc22
            2004012165

For His Dogness's buddy R. L. Whitfield

His Dogness and Lord Kelvin were out for their morning
constitutional when His Dogness spotted a heart in a ditch.
The heart wasn't the sort of heart that beats.
It was the sort of heart that feels. And it was ever-so blue.
Ever so gently His Dogness picked it up in his mouth and took
it to Lord Kelvin.

1

"Some little girl is going to be missing this," Lord Kelvin said. "But, in the meantime, let's take it with us and see what we can do about all this blueness."

He knew that it was pointless to ask the heart its address. Hearts are notoriously lax when it comes to remembering information that has numbers.

He tucked the blue heart into one of the pockets of his red plaid vest for just a moment so that he could fish around for a scrap of paper and a pen.

Finding what he needed in his trousers, he wrote a note: "Anyone missing a heart should make inquiries at His Dogness's Reading Club."

He put the note on the spot where His Dogness had found the blue heart and placed a rock on it so that it wouldn't blow away.

Lord Kelvin pulled the heart out of his vest pocket and carried it in the palm of his hand as they continued the walk.

As His Dogness sniffed memos left by other dogs and looked for signs of squirrels, Lord Kelvin speculated about what they might do to cheer up the heart. Although His Dogness doesn't say much, Lord Kelvin almost always knows what he thinks.

He thought that His Dogness's idea to take the heart for a ride in the reading club's convertible was a most-excellent one.

First, of course, they had to eat breakfast.

Hearts hardly ever eat toast or dog biscuits.

But they do eat up attention.

So, in between bites of toast for Lord Kelvin and dog biscuits for His Dogness, they lavished attention on the blue heart.

 4

After breakfast, they walked out to the convertible that they use to 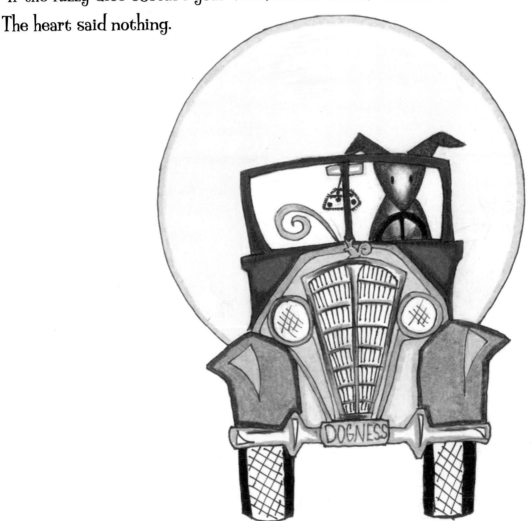 pick up the V.I.P. members of the reading club.

It is painted many bright colors and has a squirrel hood ornament.

As usual, His Dogness climbed in behind the wheel. Lord Kelvin seldom lets His Dogness drive, though, because His Dogness is subject to attacks of squirrel mania, and Lord Kelvin fears that they would end up in a ditch, not unlike the one in which they found the heart.

So Lord Kelvin made His Dogness skootch over to the passenger side. He put the heart on the seat between them.

"If the fuzzy dice obscure your view, let me know," Lord Kelvin said.

The heart said nothing.

And they were off.

First, they visited one of their favorite spots in Winston-Salem— the Old Salem historic district.

His Dogness finds the giant coffeepot amusing. They drove past it twice to make sure that the blue heart got a good look.

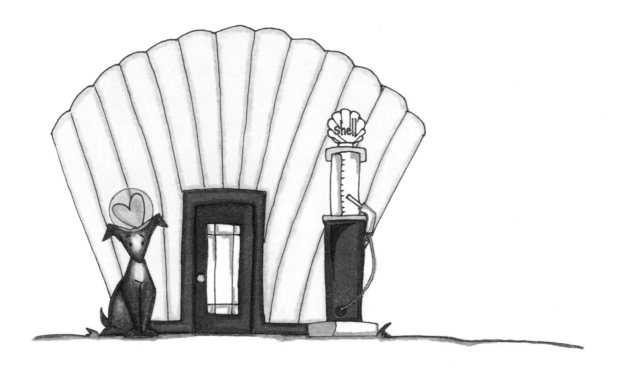

Next, they drove to the old Shell service station that looks like a shell.
Now what?

His Dogness thought that it was too bad that their friend Stan was on vacation in Antarctica. Otherwise, they could visit him. His Dogness was sure that the blue heart would enjoy sitting on Stan's helmet.

Stan is a firefighter. They met the day His Dogness spotted a squirrel right on the front porch and had such a severe bout of squirrel mania that the issue of *Dog Days* he had been perusing spontaneously combusted.

Although Stan doesn't let His Dogness drive either, he does let him mash the buttons that turn on the flashing lights and siren.

On the outskirts of town, they spotted a man on a small bulldozer. He was pushing red dirt into piles. His Dogness thought that the blue heart would enjoy riding on the bulldozer.

"That is a most-excellent idea," Lord Kelvin said.

They parked and walked over to see if the bulldozer man would be willing to give the blue heart a ride.

Although everyone can see the heart that beats, not everyone can see the heart that feels, whether it's blue or otherwise. But Lord Kelvin and His Dogness have a knack for finding just the right people—people who can see things that are invisible to others.

"This heart is blue, and we're trying to cheer it up until we find its owner," Lord Kelvin said. "His Dogness thought it might like a bulldozer ride."

"It certainly does need cheering up," he said. "It would be my pleasure to give it a ride."

He perched the heart on his yellow hardhat and drove it around and around. They made a pile of red dirt as big as a horse, although not as beautiful.

When the bulldozer man brought back the blue heart, he said, "You know, I think His Dogness had the right idea. I don't think it's quite as blue as it was."

Sure enough, it had the merest hint of purple to it around the edges.

9

When Lord Kelvin turned to congratulate His Dogness on his most-excellent idea, he was gone.

Lord Kelvin spotted him in the driver's seat of the bulldozer. The bulldozer man knew nothing of His Dogness's bouts of squirrel mania.

Still, he had reservations about His Dogness driving the bulldozer. So His Dogness climbed down.

After they drove away, they saw some people in a field flying kites. His Dogness thought that the heart might like to fly like a kite.

"That is a most-excellent idea," Lord Kelvin said.

They pulled over, and Lord Kelvin rummaged around in the trunk to see if he could find some string. The trunk of the car invariably had whatever Lord Kelvin needed and, sure enough, he found a ball of twine next to His Dogness's bowling shoes.

Lord Kelvin looped the string
around the blue heart.
Off it sailed into the sky.

LEE COUNTY LIBRARY
107 Hawkins Ave.
Sanford, NC 27330

13

His Dogness knew just how the heart felt. Sometimes, on blustery days, the wind would catch his ears, and he would soar high in the air.

When the wind was blowing, if he had another adventure already scheduled, he tried to remember to keep his ears rotated toward the ground.

The heart proved to be quite adept at figure eights. When it came down, it was looking even more not-quite-so blue.

14

Lord Kelvin thought they had time for one more adventure before lunch.
They climbed back in the car.

"Skootch over," Lord Kelvin said.

His Dogness skootched over.

They drove around some more as they looked for the next adventure to present itself.

When they drove past the Reynolda House Museum of American Art, Lord Kelvin said he didn't know why he didn't think of it before.

Next to books, art is the best balm for a blue heart.

So they drove over to see their friend Jen, who had painted many beautiful paintings for the reading club, including the one of a cow doing a one-hoofed stand that hangs in the girls' bathroom.

His Dogness rang the doorbell.

"I see you have a blue heart with you," Jen said, when she opened the door.

"Yes," Lord Kelvin said. "We found it in a ditch this morning and are having some adventures in hopes of cheering it up. We thought you might show it some of your art."

"I have another idea," Jen said. "Why don't I paint its portrait?"

"That is a most-excellent idea," Lord Kelvin said.

 16

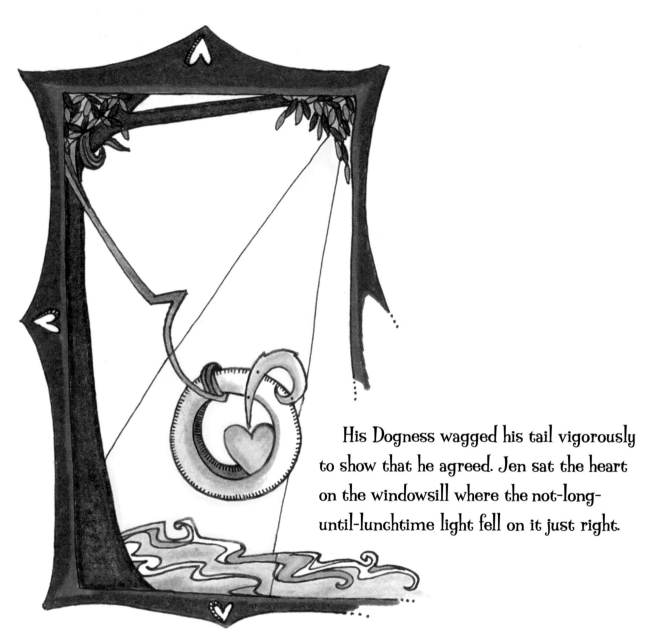

His Dogness wagged his tail vigorously to show that he agreed. Jen sat the heart on the windowsill where the not-long-until-lunchtime light fell on it just right.

She painted it swinging in a tire swing over a creek. While she painted, His Dogness and Lord Kelvin imagined they were sitting on the bank of the creek in the shade.

When Jen showed the painting to the heart, everyone was certain that it looked even more not-quite-so blue.

17

His Dogness thought it might even have a touch of red in it.

Lord Kelvin thanked Jen, and His Dogness gave her his deluxe thank-you wag.

They walked out to the car.

"Skootch over," Lord Kelvin said.

His Dogness skootched over, and they drove over to His Dogness's Reading Club for lunch. When they arrived, they didn't see the broccoli truck in the parking lot, which was good because the broccoli truck was not allowed to make deliveries.

They didn't see the Krispy Kreme doughnut truck either but that may have been because it had already come and gone.

Above the doorbell to the club was a little sign like the ones on some buildings that say "No Solicitors." Only this one said "No Broccoli."

Above the door was a quote by Antoine de Saint-Exupéry from *The Little Prince*. It said: "You become responsible, forever, for what you have tamed."

His Dogness and Lord Kelvin change the quote whenever the mood strikes them, so, when you come, you might see something else.

When Lord Kelvin went to sit in his favorite chair, which is covered in green leather, he saw that a V.I.P. member was sitting in it.

She was curled so that her legs were draped over one of the arms.

Lord Kelvin took a moment to lean over and see what she was reading. It was the latest book by Mortimer J. Pithmarrow. It was called *Eschew Obfuscation.*

"Gesundheit," Lord Kelvin said.

"Pardon me?" the V.I.P. member said.

"Nothing. Sorry to bother you. Carry on," Lord Kelvin said.

20

He walked over to his second-favorite chair. He didn't like it quite as much as his first-favorite chair because, from it, he couldn't see the fountain made of two tubas out in the garden.

It became his favorite chair for the day, though, because he found that Lydia, who brings her own chair, was reading nearby.

She showed him the illustrations in her book about the Loch Ness monster. Lydia thinks Nessie is not a monster at all, just a little shy.

Before picking out a spot to settle down in, His Dogness walked around the club to give everyone the opportunity to scritch him behind the ear.

After giving His Dogness a scritch, Julie, who handles the reading club responsibilities that His Dogness and Lord Kelvin don't feel like taking care of, went over to say hello to Lord Kelvin.

"Has anyone been making inquiries about a missing heart?" he asked.

"No," she said. "The broccoli truck man called again, though. He wanted to know whether he could bring some broccoli to the club if he smothered it in tangy cheese sauce."

"You have to admire his stick-to-it-iveness," Lord Kelvin said. "But you, of course, told him 'no.' "

"Of course. Where did you find the blue heart?"

"His Dogness found it in a ditch when we were taking our morning constitutional. It was ever-so blue. We have been taking it on adventures in hopes of cheering it up."

"It looks as if it's working," Julie said. "It definitely looks not-quite-so-blue now."

"Yes, but I hope we find its owner soon. Although some people go around without their hearts for ages, I don't think it's a good idea at all."

His Dogness and Lord Kelvin ate lunch. In the following days, they ate many more lunches without anyone making inquiries about a lost heart.

The broccoli truck man did make inquiries, though, about whether he might possibly bring over a broccoli casserole made using his Aunt Sue's recipe.

It was a measure of how distracted Lord Kelvin was by the blue-heart business that he almost said "yes" by accident.

23

Luckily, he came to his senses in time. Escaping from his close call perked him up a bit but that had but worn off by the time Ann-Mikel dropped by and found him sitting in his favorite chair.

His Dogness was off being scritched by a V.I.P. member taking a break from reading *Tragedy on the Cliff* by Eileen Dover.

"How's it going?" Ann-Mikel asked.

"Swimmingly," Lord Kelvin said, "except I fear that our story of the not-quite-so-blue heart might not have a happy ending. We still haven't found the girl it belongs to."

"Nonsense," Ann-Mikel said. "You're just looking in the wrong place for the happy ending. This time it came at the beginning when you and His Dogness found the heart in the ditch.

Who knows what might have become of that heart if you hadn't come along? Look at it now."

24

Lord Kelvin looked out the window. The heart was riding atop the water spouting out of the double-tuba fountain.

"You're right," he said. "This story does already have one happy ending. Maybe it will have another one some day when we find the little girl."

Lord Kelvin extracted himself from his chair and went over to open the door to the garden so that His Dogness could go out.

His Dogness had seen a squirrel that needed chasing up a tree, and he was eager to oblige.

26

LEE COUNTY LIBRARY
107 Hawkins Ave.
Sanford, NC 27330

14

LEE COUNTY LIBRARY SYSTEM
DISCARD
3 3262 00283 7331